Billie B. Brown

www.BillieBBrownBooks.com

Billie B. Brown Books

The Bad Butterfly
The Soccer Star
The Midnight Feast
The Second-best Friend
The Extra-special Helper
The Beautiful Haircut
The Big Sister
The Spotty Vacation
The Birthday Mix-up
The Secret Message
The Little Lie
The Best Project
The Deep End
The Copycat Kid
The Night Fright
The Bully Buster
The Missing Tooth
The Book Buddies

First American Edition 2020
Kane Miller, A Division of EDC Publishing
Original Title: Billie B Brown: The Bully Buster
Text Copyright © 2012 Sally Rippin
Illustration Copyright © 2012 Aki Fukuoka
Logo and Design Copyright © 2012 Hardie Grant Egmont
First published in Australia by Hardie Grant Egmont

For information contact:
Kane Miller, A Division of EDC Publishing
P.O. Box 470663
Tulsa, OK 74147-0663
www.kanemiller.com
www.edcpub.com
www.usbornebooksandmore.com

Library of Congress Control Number: 2019951187

Printed and bound in the United States of America
3 4 5 6 7 8 9 10
ISBN: 978-1-68464-132-1

The Bully Buster

By Sally Rippin

Illustrated by Aki Fukuoka

Kane Miller
A DIVISION OF EDC PUBLISHING

Chapter One

Billie B. Brown has
one lumpy schoolbag,
two banana sandwiches
and one grumpy frown.
Do you want to know
what the "B" in Billie B.
Brown stands for?

Bully.

There is a big bully at Billie's school. His name is Jason. He is in grade five. Yesterday Billie and Jack were playing on the field with Billie's new soccer ball. Jason walked past and **kicked** the soccer ball up, up, up into the peppercorn tree.

2

One grumpy frown

One lumpy schoolbag

Two banana sandwiches

3

"Hey, that's my soccer ball!" Billie said.

"So?" said Jason **meanly**. Then he poked Billie in the shoulder. "If you tell on me, there'll be BIG trouble. OK?"

Billie bit her lip and nodded her head. She had never been this close to Jason before. He was scary.

Jason **stomped** away.

Billie felt tears sting her eyes. "That was my new ball," she said in a little voice.

"We should tell Ms. Walton," Jack said.

"No!" said Billie. "You heard what Jason said. If he finds out we've told on him, there will be BIG trouble."

So the ball stayed in the tree and Billie and Jack walked glumly back to class.

Today, Billie is prepared. She and Jack have decided they are not going to play on the field anymore. Billie doesn't want to bump into that horrible Jason again.

Billie and Jack's first class is art. Billie loves art. This week their class has been making teapots out of clay for Mother's Day. The clay has been drying overnight, so today they are ready for painting.

Jack's teapot is shaped like a robot. It has one arm for the handle and one for the spout. It is a very good robot teapot.

Billie is trying to make a teapot house.

But it is not quite turning out how she had hoped. Right now it looks more like something from an elephant's bottom.

Billie giggles.

"Would you like some elephant poop tea, sir?" she says in a posh voice.

Jack giggles too.
Then they both hum the teapot song until the bell goes for recess.

Chapter Two

Ms. Walton tells everyone to take their teapots straight to the classroom. Then they can go out to play.

Billie and Jack pick up

their teapots and carry
them carefully out of the
art room. Even though
Billie's teapot looks a bit
funny, she knows that her
mom will love it.

On their way back to class, Billie sees Rebecca by the monkey bars. She decides she will quickly show Rebecca her teapot. She knows it will make Rebecca laugh.

"I'm just going to see Rebecca," Billie says to Jack.

"But Ms. Walton said…" Jack says, looking worried.

Billie huffs. "I won't be long!"

She walks carefully over to the monkey bars.

Rebecca sees Billie and waves. Billie walks faster. She has nearly reached Rebecca when... **crash!** Someone runs into Billie. Her teapot goes smashing to the ground.

Rebecca gasps. Billie gasps.
She looks up. There,
standing in front of her,
is Jason! He is red cheeked
and puffing.

Billie feels a hot ball of **anger** rush into her chest. She doesn't care that Jason is the biggest, meanest bully in the whole school. He has broken her teapot and that is NOT FAIR!

"Look what you've done!" she yells loudly. "You broke my teapot!

You kicked my soccer ball into the tree. You are the meanest, **horriblest** person ever. And NOBODY LIKES YOU!"

When Billie finishes yelling, her head is fizzing. Jason's mouth drops open and he runs away.

Rebecca kneels down and helps Billie pick up the pieces of her teapot. "He didn't even say sorry," Billie says **angrily**. "I bet he did it on purpose!"

"You should tell Ms. Walton," Rebecca says.

Billie shakes her head. "That will only make it worse," she says. "Jason is horrible and mean, but he is scary too."

"He looked more scared than scary when you yelled at him like that!" Rebecca says.

Billie laughs. But deep down, she feels **worried**. Will Jason be angry at her? She walks back to class with the pieces of broken teapot in her hands.

Chapter Three

When Ms. Walton sees Billie's teapot, she looks surprised. "Oh dear, Billie!" she says. "What happened?"

"I dropped it," says Billie quietly.

She feels bad lying to
Ms. Walton, but she can't
think of what else to say.

"Never mind. You can still do a drawing for Mother's Day," Ms. Walton says. "But that's why you should have come straight back to the classroom!"

Billie nods. If she had come straight back she never would have bumped into that horrible Jason.

Billie and Jack play on the monkey bars with Rebecca all recess. But only after they check that Jason is nowhere to be seen.

"Why was Jason over by the monkey bars, anyway?" Billie says. "He never usually comes over to our side of the playground."

"I hope he doesn't come over here again!" Jack says **nervously**.

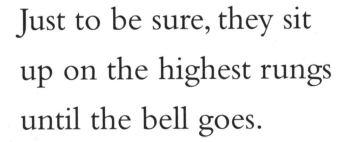

Just to be sure, they sit up on the highest rungs until the bell goes.

In class, Billie works hard on her math. She finishes her work early so that she has time to draw a picture for Mother's Day. She draws her mom standing under a rainbow. It is much nicer than her lumpy teapot. But she is still annoyed that Jason broke it.

The bell goes for
lunch break. Jack packs
up quickly. Billie is still
finishing her drawing.

"Meet you at the
monkey bars?" Jack says.

Billie nods. She finishes her drawing as everyone goes outside to play. She rolls it up and carries it out to her bag in the corridor.

Billie unzips her bag and puts the drawing in. Just then, she hears footsteps. She spins around. Someone is standing right in front of her.

You know who it is,
don't you? That's right.
It's Jason! Billie's heart
begins to jump around
in her chest like a
frightened rabbit.

Chapter Four

"Wh...wh...what do you want?" Billie says, trying to sound brave. She wishes she hadn't shouted at Jason. She is sure she is in trouble.

Jason frowns. "Hey, pip-squeak. I've got something for you," he says in a gruff voice. Then he brings Billie's soccer ball out from behind his back.

Billie looks surprised. "How did you get *that?*"

Jason shrugs. "I came to school last night with my dad. We got it down with a broomstick." He grins. "Lucky he's tall."

"Oh," Billie says. Is Jason being *nice* to her? The big mean bully?

"Um, thank you," she
says shyly.

"I was coming over to
tell you I had it at recess,"
Jason says. "When…you
know…when I bumped
into you. And you
dropped your…what
was that thing again?"

"A teapot," says Billie,
feeling **annoyed**.

Jason kicks at the floor. "Anyway, it's true what you said. That nobody likes me."

"Really?" Billie asks. She can't imagine what it must feel like to have no friends. It must be very lonely.

Jason looks down at his grubby fingers. "I'm no good at games.

I get angry and then I
mess everything up.
Now no one wants
to play with me."

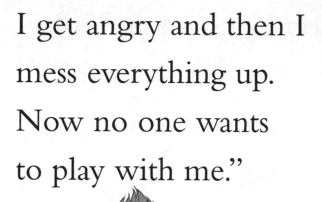

"So?" says Billie. "I get
angry sometimes too."

Jason grins. "I know you
do!"

"But I still have friends," says Billie. "If you mess up, you just have to say sorry."

Jason goes quiet for a while. Then he gets a funny look on his face. A little bit like he has something sticky and **chewy** in his mouth.

"Erm…sorry about your soccer ball," he says quietly. "And your teapot."

Billie feels the hot, angry ball inside her chest soften.

"That's all right," she says. "It wasn't a very good teapot anyway. Actually, it was more like an elephant poop than a teapot."

Jason laughs loudly. When he laughs, he doesn't look so mean anymore. He puts his big hand on Billie's shoulder. "You're all right," he says. "For a pip-squeak."

Billie grins. "You're all right, too. For a bully."

Jason laughs again. Even louder this time. Billie realizes he's not so bad, after all.

Just then, Billie has an idea. A super-duper idea. "Hey, do you like to play soccer?" she asks.

"Yep!" says Jason proudly. Then his face drops. "But no one wants me on their team."

"Well, do you want to play with us?" says Billie.

"Really?" says Jason **excitedly**.

"Sure. But no more kicking the ball into the tree, OK?" she says sternly.

41

"Or there'll be BIG trouble."

Jason grins. "OK," he says. "I promise."

Billie grins too. She can't wait to see the look on Jack's face when she walks into the playground with the big bully.

Billie B. Brown — The Bad Butterfly — By Sally Rippin

Billie B. Brown — The Soccer Star — By Sally Rippin

Billie B. Brown — The Midnight Feast — By Sally Rippin

Billie B. Brown — The Second-best Friend — By Sally Rippin

Billie B. Brown — The Extra-special Helper — By Sally Rippin

Billie B. Brown — The Beautiful Haircut — By Sally Rippin

Billie B. Brown — The Big Sister — By Sally Rippin

Billie B. Brown — The Spotty Vacation — By Sally Rippin

Billie B. Brown — The Birthday Mix-up — By Sally Rippin

Billie B. Brown — The Secret Message — By Sally Rippin

Billie B. Brown — The Little Lie — By Sally Rippin

Billie B. Brown — The Best Project — By Sally Rippin

Billie B. Brown — The Deep End — By Sally Rippin

Billie B. Brown — The Copycat Kid — By Sally Rippin

Billie B. Brown — The Night Fright — By Sally Rippin

Billie B. Brown — The Missing Tooth — By Sally Rippin

Billie B. Brown — The Bully Buster — By Sally Rippin

Billie B. Brown & Hey Jack! — The Book Buddies — By Sally Rippin

Collect them all!
Including a new title starring both Jack AND Bill